The Most Wonderful Egg in the World

in the World

written and illustrated by **Helme Heine**

Für Fabian

A Margaret K. McElderry Book

Atheneum   *New York*

Once upon a time, a long time ago, three hens were quarreling about which of them was the most beautiful.

Dotty had the most beautiful feathers.

Stalky had the most beautiful legs.

And Plumy had the most beautiful crest.

Since they could not settle their quarrel among themselves, they decided to ask the king for his advice.

"What you can do is more important than what you look like," said the king. "Whichever one of you lays the most wonderful egg I will make a princess."

He went out into the palace park followed by all the hens in his kingdom.

Dotty preened her beautiful feathers before settling herself in the wet grass. It was not long before she cackled, stood up, and stepped aside.

Everybody was speechless. There lay an egg, snow-white, spotless, and perfectly shaped—the eggshell shimmering like polished marble. "This is the most perfect egg I have ever seen," cried the king, and all the hens nodded.

Then it was Stalky's turn. Everybody felt a little sorry for her. They knew she could not lay a more perfect egg. It was impossible.

After ten minutes Stalky cackled, got up and
stretched her legs proudly in the morning sun.

The king clapped his hands for joy. There lay an
egg of such size and weight that even an ostrich
would have been jealous.

"This is the biggest egg I have ever seen," cried the king, and all the hens nodded.

While they were still nodding, Plumy settled herself carefully on the ground. Everybody felt extremely sorry for her. They knew she could not lay a more perfect or bigger egg. It was unthinkable. Modestly, with castdown eyes, she sat there.

Then, with only a small cackle, she got up to reveal
an egg that would be talked about for the next
hundred years.

Before them lay a square egg. Each side was straight,
as if drawn with a ruler, and each surface shone in a
different color.

"This is indeed the most fantastic egg I have ever
seen," cried the king, and all the hens nodded.

It was impossible to say which egg was the most wonderful. So the king decided that all three hens— Dotty, Stalky and Plumy—should be made princesses.

And from that day to this they have been the best of friends, and have happily gone on laying extraordinary eggs.